Rhiannon

Katy Cawkwell started telling tales to those around her while walking over the Scottish hills by day and huddled at the side of campfires by night. She has been performing as a storyteller in the theatres and festivals, clubs and pubs of Britain and beyond since 1996. She first stepped into the world of the *Mabinogion* as a child, through an illustrated book of *Culhwch and Olwen*, inventing her own band of special heroes to come with her on her travels. More recently, she has returned to the first and third branches of the *Mabinogion* and the Welsh landscape in which they are rooted, resulting in an oral and now a written retelling of the story of Rhiannon.

Peter Bodenham is a visual artist. His work includes large scale installation pieces, walking projects and small scale drawings. He has been known to walk to London from Cardigan with a stuffed goose as part of the 2MPH project and is part of the Ointment art group. He lives in west Wales.

The story of Rhiannon

retold by
Katy Cawkwell

PARTHIAN

Parthian
The Old Surgery
Napier Street
Cardigan
SA43 1ED

www.parthianbooks.co.uk

First published in 2007
© Katy Cawkwell 2007
All Rights Reserved

ISBN 978-1-905762-34-7

Editor: Jeff Teare

Cover design and typesetting by Lucy Llewellyn
Cover image and illustrations by Peter Bodenham

Printed and bound by Dinefwr Press, Llandybïe, Wales

The publisher acknowledges the financial support of the
Welsh Books Council.

British Library Cataloguing in Publication Data

A cataloguing record for this book is available from the
British Library.

For Kamlesh

Prologue

I was standing in a wood of silver birch trees. The sun was streaming in and when I turned my face to it, the light was almost blinding and the trees were dark, silhouetted against the sky. But when I looked the other way, the pale bark gleamed against the dark blue of a late summer sky. Dark on light, light on dark. Image and negative. Was I standing in two worlds or one? It all depends on how you look at it.

I was walking along a path. I came to a pool where dark trees hung over the surface of the water. It was a strange place and I was sure I'd never been there before, until, all at once, I realised that it was so familiar and I'd been there so many times before, but every other time, I'd come walking along the path in the other direction. One path or two? It all depends on how you look at it.

Imagine now, that our whole land is like this – the woods and the rivers, the hills and the valleys – all of it, two worlds, one layered upon the other. Imagine that there are some places where it is easier to peel back this world and to look through into another world, the Otherworld. One of these places is a hill in the south-west corner of Wales. The sides are rounded, sloping smoothly away on every side, the grass nibbled short by the ponies, but the hill is topped with a jagged crown of rock, silhouetted against the sky.

Í

A young man rode up the slopes of the hill. He looped the reins over the rock, scrambled to the top and sat there, wedged in among the bluestone rock, with the land falling away beneath him. He looked out at the slope of the hill, the fields beyond, the little farms and the houses, the men and animals working on the land. Further out, he could see the tower of a castle rising from a little town and in the far distance, the glimmer of the sea.

The land spread out below him was the kingdom of Dyfed and the young man was Pwyll, king of Dyfed. He was looking out over his land, at the castle where he held his court and he had come up onto the hill with a purpose. There was an old saying:

> 'If a king of Dyfed shall sit upon the hill,
> Not undertaking it lightly,

If a man of noble blood shall sit upon the hill,
Putting his life into the land,
It will reward him with a blessing,
Or curse him with a great blow.'

'A blessing or a curse,' thought Pwyll, 'which will it be?'

He gazed out hopefully. A golden haze began to move and shift across the land, blocking it out from his view. It drew closer, until the brightness, whiteness was all around him. He peered out, willing it to part, and as he looked, it shifted again, revealing the side of the hill.

On the hillside, he saw a great white horse, walking slowly away from him. On the horse, a woman sat tall and straight, as if she'd grown from the horse's back, with her golden hair trailing down over green robes. Above her head, there were three birds singing.

Pwyll didn't dare take his eyes off her. He went scrambling backwards over the rocks, reaching for his horse. He swung himself into the saddle, pulled the reins free, and walked after her, thinking to come alongside. But the woman walked round the side of the hill a little bit ahead of him. Pwyll frowned. He didn't seem to be gaining any ground, so he dug his heels into the horse's sides and urged him into a trot. But still the woman walked on, always that little bit ahead of him. Pwyll kicked the horse again and now they were galloping round the hill, the horse's mane streaming out, his sides wet with sweat and Pwyll himself red in the face, eyes popping with the effort of the ride. But the woman on the horse moved slowly on, not a golden hair, not a green sleeve out of place, always that little bit ahead of him.

They came right round the hillside and Pwyll was desperate, he thought he might lose her altogether and so at last he cried out,

'Lady! For the sake of the man you love best, will you not stop and turn to me?'

At once, the horse stopped and the woman turned to face him.

'At last!' she said, 'I thought you'd never ask.'

She looked Pwyll up and down and at his horse, steaming with the exertion of the ride.

'And Pwyll,' she said, 'Lord of Dyfed. Next time, for the sake of your horse if not your own self, ask me a little sooner!'

Pwyll stared at her.

'You know my name,' he said. 'Tell me, what is yours and what is your business on this hillside?'

'I am Rhiannon,' she said. 'And our paths have crossed many times before. You in your world and I in mine. I watched you from my world, although you could never see me. When I first saw you, my heart went out to you and the more I watched you, the more I loved you. And perhaps it would have stayed like this, with me watching from a distance... only now I am in trouble in my own world and so it is to you I have come. Pwyll, I have come to ask for your help, your protection.

'In my own world, I am pledged to marry a man I do not love. He is the Grey Lord. He cannot smile, his heart is barren, he cannot love me. And yet he binds me to his side, an object of beauty, and I cannot free myself from his grasp. The wedding feast is a year from today, on the eve of summer. Pwyll, will you come to that feast and rescue me, and make that wedding feast our own?'

Pwyll just went on staring at her. He had come up onto the hill, hoping for a blessing, and here was the most beautiful woman he'd ever seen, offering him love with one hand and adventure with the other: it doesn't take more to make a young man speechless.

'Rhiannon,' he said at last, 'whatever I have to do I will do it. Just tell me how.'

'Good,' she said, 'listen then.' She took a jar of ointment and a little bag from her robes, she gave them to him and she told him exactly what he had to do. Pwyll took the jar and the bag and he agreed to what she said.

'Are you sure about this?' she said at last.

'I'm sure I'm sure,' said Pwyll. He watched as she turned from him and walked away round the side of the hill. First the horse, then the woman and lastly the three birds singing, disappeared into the hillside. Pwyll rubbed his eyes, but they were truly gone, vanished into the hill. Had it all been a vision? He looked down. There was the little bag, there was the ointment. He put them in his own bag and he rode back down the hill, back across the land to his castle.

íí

Pwyll walked through that year as if in a dream. Rhiannon's face was always before his eyes, her voice echoing in his ears. The seasons turned, the year passed and the eve of summer came round once more. Pwyll made himself ready and then he summoned his nine truest friends, his most trusted companions.

'Tonight I ride to my wedding feast. Will you ride with me?'

And so Pwyll and his men rode out at twilight across the land until they came to the foot of the hill. They tethered the horses and began to climb the rock-ridden, pony-nibbled slopes. Pwyll was looking for the place where Rhiannon had disappeared into the hill and when he found it, he drew out the jar of ointment. He smeared the ointment over the eyes of his men and lastly over his own eyes. When they opened their eyes, they stared in amazement. There was the hillside with the jagged crown of rock above them, but layered across their world was another world: a silver arch, with a silver path leading through, lush grass on either side. Even the stars seemed to have shifted in their patterns in the sky.

'This is it!' said Pwyll. 'Follow me.' He stepped through the silver arch, set his foot on the silver path and the nine trusted companions followed close behind him. They gazed around them at the new world. A white hare with red ears sprang away from them through the grass and it wasn't long before they came to a great hall with the door closed to them.

'This is the place,' said Pwyll. He unclasped the brooch at his throat, took off the cloak of a king and underneath he was wearing the rags of a beggar. He took the little bag that Rhiannon had given him and turned to his men:
'You must wait here, but come when I call and come quickly!'
Then he turned to the door and knocked.

The door was opened by a man with eyes as blue as the summer sky, little creases and crinkles round the corners. He looked neither pleased nor displeased to see Pwyll, he simply swung the door on its hinge and let him in. Pwyll came into the great vaulted feasting hall. There was a long table, spread with a wedding feast and either side, the wedding guests sat on long benches.

Pwyll looked up and saw the woman he had come for at the head of the table. More lovely than he'd remembered, Rhiannon sat with her eyes cast down, her lips pressed tight together and he saw then the reason why: sitting by her side was a man with a pale, shadowy face, without the shiver of a smile and dark hair, striped with silver like a badger, the Grey Lord himself. Pwyll shuddered when he saw him, but he remembered what he had to do and edged forward down the hall until he stood at the elbow of the Lord.

8

He stretched out his little bag.

'Please sir,' he said, 'it's a good day for you. Will you make it a good day for me and fill this little bag?'

The Grey Lord looked down from the table.

'Very well,' he said, 'you don't ask for much with a bag that size.' He took the bag, reached for some bread and cheese and put it in the bag, but it wasn't quite full, so he took more food – meat and fish – and he put them in the bag, but it still wasn't quite full. The Grey Lord frowned and he reached out for more – fruit and cake and nuts – but when he looked, the little bag was still not quite full. He looked down crossly at Pwyll.

'Will this bag ever be full?'

'No sir. Not until a man of noble blood puts his feet into the bag and tramples down the feast.'

'I'm not doing that!'

But at that point, Rhiannon raised her face, put her hand on the Grey Lord's arm and said,

'Come, do as the beggar asks and then we can be rid of him.'

So the Grey Lord got down from the table, took the little bag in his hands and stepped one foot and then the other foot into the bag. At once, Rhiannon took one side, Pwyll took the other, they lifted it up and over his head and Pwyll tied the mouth of the bag tight. He gave a whistle, a call for his men and they came running into the court. Pwyll picked up the bag and he threw it to them.

'There's a beast in the bag!' he cried. 'A badger in the bag! Beat the beast, beat the badger till he cries!'

The men took sticks and they began to beat the bag, until the Grey Lord cried out for mercy:

'I'll give you whatever you want, only stop and set me free!'

'That's all I wanted to hear,' said Pwyll. 'Set him free!'

The men untied the mouth of the bag and the Grey Lord stood up, the food and the filth of the feast falling away from him. He stepped clear of the bag and he stood there, unblemished, unbruised, unhurt. He turned to Pwyll,

'What is it that you want from me?'

'I want what I came for: Rhiannon
and the wedding feast.'

When the Grey Lord heard that,
he turned to Rhiannon,

'This is your choice, is it?'

'This is my choice.'

'It is a poor choice. You are choosing to leave a world where you are ever-young, ever-beautiful. A world where we spread the tables like this.' He waved his hand and at once the table was laden with a fresh wedding feast. 'You are leaving all this, to go with that man there? To go to a world where you will suffer, you will grow old and Death will take those you love from you. It is a poor choice.'

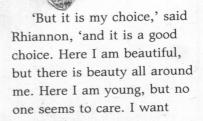

'But it is my choice,' said Rhiannon, 'and it is a good choice. Here I am beautiful, but there is beauty all around me. Here I am young, but no one seems to care. I want

to suffer, so that I feel the happiness that comes when suffering is over. I want to grow old, so that while I am young, every moment is precious. But most of all I follow my heart, I go for love of this man.'

She took Pwyll by the hand and they walked together down the hall. The man with the eyes as blue as the summer sky got up and opened the door for them. The Grey Lord turned to watch them go and he raised a hand after them:

'Go then. But I curse your going. My vengeance will linger with you wherever you go and my memory is long.'

The two of them shuddered, as they stood in the arch of the door, but they did not look behind them. They set their feet onto the silver path and they walked away, with the nine companions close behind. They came to the silver arch and Pwyll turned to Rhiannon.

'Are you sure about this?'

'I'm sure I'm sure,' she said. She looked resolutely straight ahead of her, took a deep breath and stepped through the silver arch.

That is how Rhiannon came from her world into our own, how she became wife of Pwyll and Queen of Dyfed.

ííí

Rhiannon threw herself into this world with a passion for doing and feeling and being what before she had only seen, watching between the worlds, as if from a great distance.

She learnt how corn is planted in the dark earth,
  How to tell when apples are ripe for picking,
  How to boil the sugar for jam,
  How to knead the dough for bread,
  How to sew up her dresses if they were torn,
  How to touch up her eyes if they were tired.

The three birds that had once circled and sung above her head now fluttered inside of her, and they were learning new songs:
  The tune of the workmen in the fields,
  The rhythm and hum of the spinning wheel by the fire,

The quickening heartbeat of a mortal woman.

Rhiannon learnt how to tell the time of day by the way the sun moves across the sky,
How to feel in her bones when the rain was coming,
And how to talk about the weather for hours on end!

Above all, she learnt what it was to be a queen of Dyfed and she felt the weight of the expectation of her people upon her shoulders. And the greatest expectation of all was for a child.

But the seasons turned, the years went by, and there was no child.

The people of Dyfed began to murmur and mutter,
'This beautiful queen from the Otherworld – was she really a blessing or rather a curse? If she is barren and without a child, our land will not bear fruit.'

At last, the muttering grew so loud that the nine companions came to Pwyll. They stood around him and made him listen,
'You chose poorly, Pwyll. You chose a woman from another world to be your wife and now she will not bear you a child. You must get rid of her, send her back where she came from and choose a woman from your own world.'
Pwyll felt the rage boiling up inside him and he glared back at them.
'How dare you ask this of me? Rhiannon has done nothing wrong. You and the people will have to be patient.'

He sent them away, but the anger stayed with him and this was partly because what they had said to him echoed what he had caught himself feeling, deep in his own heart. Still angry, he went

out to the stables and took his horse. He let the reins hang loose, let
the horse take him where he chose, not caring as the young
branches snapped against his face. They came out into a clearing
where a river tumbled down over the rocks into a dark pool and
flowed sunlit, away through the trees. Pwyll sighed and at last he
got down from his horse, knelt by the
pool and drank deeply from the cool
water. When he looked up, he gave
a start. There, on the opposite
bank, stood a familiar stranger,
leaning on a staff and looking at
him with eyes as blue as the
summer sky, little crinkles and
creases round the corners:

'Is there trouble in the kingdom,
Pwyll, Lord of Dyfed?'

Pwyll hesitated and then he found himself pouring out his trouble, the worry that gnawed at his heart: the lack of a child.

'It seems,' said the stranger, 'that your horse knew more than you did yourself, because he has brought you to the right place. They say that in this pool there swims a silver fish. They say that if a man should catch that fish with his own hands, the flesh of that fish will make the barren bear fruit.'

Pwyll gazed into the pool and sure enough, there was the glint of a fish deep beneath the surface. He looked back at the stranger, but he had vanished as quickly as he had come. 'It can do no harm,' he thought. 'And perhaps it will do some good.'

He eased his hand into the water, letting the fish come to him, and when he felt the silver scales against his fingers, he flicked his wrist and the fish shot out of the water onto the bank. Pwyll pounced on it and struck its head with a stone. He took a knife from his belt and cut off the fish's head and the fish's tail and he threw them into the river. Next he slit the fish down the middle and he washed the guts and the blood away into the water. Then he wrapped the flesh of the fish in a cloth and put it in his bag.

The river took the head and the tail and the guts of the fish and carried them downstream, to where the river widened out into the sea. They washed up on the shore and a white mare, grazing on the kelp, munched up the head and the tail and the guts of that silver fish.

Pwyll rode back to the castle with purpose. He'd never cooked a fish before, but he was determined to do it himself, so he pushed the cook to one side, stoked up the fire, took a frying pan, unwrapped the flesh of the fish and turned it this way and that until it was perfectly done. He slid it onto a plate and carried it in his own hands to Rhiannon.

She smiled as he set it before her: Pwyll had never cooked her anything before! She ate it all up, leaving only the skin and a few scraps, and she said it was delicious. When she was done, she laid the plate on the ground and one of the white hunting dogs ran up and licked it clean.

íʊ

Perhaps it was patience, or perhaps there was wisdom in the words of the stranger with eyes as blue as the summer sky: as the weeks went by, Rhiannon's waist thickened and quickened with life, until nine months later, she was full to bursting, on the brink of birth. It was a great occasion and so not one midwife, but six royal midwives were summoned from all over Dyfed to attend her. When the time came, they took her to her room and they were there with her as she gave birth to a little baby boy. They cooed over the child, washed him, wrapped him in a silken cloth and laid him on his mother's breast.

Rhiannon looked down at her child, a great smile spread over her face, and in that smile, all the worry, all the waiting, all the struggle were washed away. She felt a new kind of happiness. Relief and joy overwhelmed her, she lay back with the baby on her breast, and she fell fast asleep.

The six midwives settled themselves down on a bench, leaning up against the wall, and watched the mother and child asleep. It had been a long, exhausting day for them too. The first midwife yawned, soon her head lolled and she was fast asleep, leaning up against the second midwife. The second midwife made herself a little more comfortable, but she just couldn't keep her eyes open any longer and soon her head drooped to one side, sleeping on the shoulder of the third midwife. The third slept on the shoulder of the fourth, the fourth on the fifth, the fifth on the sixth and finally the sixth midwife slept, leaning her head against the frame of the open window.

It was the sixth who woke first. A cold blast of air from the window, something moving against her cheek and she jerked herself upright. And as soon as she woke, the fifth woke too and the fifth woke the fourth, the fourth the third, the second, the first: in a moment, all six midwives were wide awake and staring in horror, because there lay Rhiannon, sleeping soundly, but the child had vanished.

'We should never have slept!' said the first midwife.
'We should have kept watch,' said the second.
'What will they say?' said the third.
'What will they do?' said the fourth.
'We'll pay for this,' said the fifth.
'Yes,' said the sixth, 'we'll pay for this with our lives.'

'What are we going to do?' said the first.
'I don't know,' said the second.
'Let's run!' said the third.
'Let's hide!' said the fourth.
'But they'll find us,' said the fifth.
'Yes,' said the sixth, 'what we need is a story – I know, we'll tell them that she killed her own child!'

'Killed her own child?' said the first.
'She'd never do that!' said the second.
'They'd never believe us!' said the third.
'Where's the blood?' said the fourth.
'Where's the body?' said the fifth.
'Listen then,' said the sixth, 'she killed her own child and ate him.'

'Ate her own child?' said the first.
'She'd never do that!' said the second.
'They'd never believe us!' said the third.
'But it is our word against theirs...' said the fourth.
'Six voices to one...' said the fifth.
'Yes,' said the sixth, looking round at each of them, 'if we all swear it.'

The midwives looked at each other and they made their terrible oath. One of them slipped down to the kitchen. A white hunting dog had given birth that very night to a pair of puppies: one was healthy and strong, the other a little runt. She snatched up the little runt puppy that should never have been born from its place by the fire and she dashed its head against the hearth stone. Cradling the body in her hands, she carried it up to the bedroom and there the six midwives took the puppy and tore him apart. They smeared the puppy's blood on Rhiannon's hands, they smeared the puppy's blood on Rhiannon's mouth, they took the puppy's flesh and scattered it over the bed and they took the puppy's little bones and broke them and scattered them over the bed. They washed their own hands, tore their own hair and screamed to wake the dead.

Rhiannon woke. Pwyll and the nine companions woke and came banging at the door. Pwyll burst in and saw Rhiannon lying bloody on the bed, with the six midwives holding her down and screaming. He looked around, looked into her eyes.

'Where's the child?' he cried. 'Where's my son?'

Rhiannon clutched at the emptiness on her breast and gasped. 'Gone!' she cried. 'Child of my heart, gone from my side!'

But the midwives pressed in on her, pointing their fingers.

'You killed him,' said the first.

'You tore his limbs,' said the second

'You drank his blood,' said the third.

'You ate his flesh,' said the fourth.

'You broke his bones,' said the fifth.

'You're a monster,' said the sixth. 'You devoured your own child!'

'No!' cried Rhiannon. 'It's not true, it isn't so, it's not...'

Just then, she tasted the blood on her lips, looked down and saw the blood on her hands. She was confused, she didn't remember clearly and a great wave of doubt and horror welled up inside her: had she done what they said she had done?

She looked desperately up at Pwyll and he looked back at her. He didn't know whether to believe that one silent voice or the six screaming ones. The nine companions, however, knew exactly what to believe and seized their chance to press in around him.

'Pwyll,' they said, 'this woman, this beast has destroyed your child, devoured your son. She has behaved like an animal and she must be treated like an animal. And we're telling you now – if you do not punish her, the people of this land will tear her apart.'

Pwyll, torn in two, stood there and said nothing. He let them drag her from the bed, bloody as she was. He said nothing and he did nothing. They took her down to the gates of the town and when morning came, they brought a bridle and fastened it over her head, took a saddle and strapped it onto her back. Her punishment was to stand by the town gates and every time a stranger came to the town, she would have to come forward and tell her story:

'I killed my own child. With these hands I tore his limbs, with these lips I drank his blood, with these teeth I ate his flesh, with these hands I broke his bones. I devoured my own child.'

She would have to offer her back to the stranger and let him ride her through the town, wherever he chose to go.

She sat there day after day, eaten away with doubt, believing and not believing the story that she told. She sat there in the heat and dust of summer, the wind and rain of winter. At night, she would crawl into the royal stables and curl up in the straw. Sometimes, Pwyll would come and open the top half of the stable door and look down at her lying there. But it was as if a cold chasm had opened up between them and there was no way that he could reach across to her.

The seasons turned, the years passed, Rhiannon's golden hair became streaked with grey and her face began to show the lines of suffering upon it. And there were times, as she staggered through the town with some great stranger riding her, when she struggled to remember why it was she had wanted to suffer, why it was she had chosen to grow old.

O

One day, three strangers came to the town: a husband and wife and between them, riding on a young white horse, a little, golden-haired boy. Rhiannon saw them coming and she shuffled out to meet them. In a flat voice, broken by the years of punishment, she told her story:

'I killed my own child. With these hands I tore his limbs, with these lips I drank his blood, with these teeth I ate his flesh, with these hands I broke his bones. I devoured my own child. Will you ride on my back through the town?'

But the man just looked straight at her.
'I don't believe your story,' he said, 'and I will not ride on the back of a queen.'
Rhiannon turned to the woman, but she just shook her head.
She turned last to the little boy, but he stared at her, fascinated.

'Uh-uh,' he said at last, shaking his head with emphasis.

When Rhiannon heard that, a tear traced down through the dirt on her cheek.

'Oh!' she cried, 'Your little boy is just the age I imagine my own child would have been, were he still alive. It would be a pleasure and an honour, if I could carry him through the town.' She reached up and lifted the boy from the horse, she held him against her breast and carried him through the town, following behind the man and the woman, with the young white horse walking behind them all.

They made their way through the town until they came to the castle gates. Pwyll himself came down to let them in and stared when he saw Rhiannon with a little golden-haired child in her arms. She came in behind the strangers and sat by the fire. As soon as she had placed the child by the fire, a young white hunting dog ran up and licked the boy's hand.

Pwyll dragged himself away from the sight of his wife with a child and back to his visitors.

'Strangers are always welcome in my house,' he said. 'But tell me, do you have some business here?'

'We have come with a story,' replied the man, 'a story that needs to be heard.'

'Good,' said Pwyll, 'stories are always welcome, in good times and troubled ones. Let's hear your tale!'

The man stepped forward and began to speak.

'My wife and I, we live two days' journey from here, down by the sea. We have a farm, a bit of land, animals – horses, mainly – but a few years ago, what we longed for most of all, we did not have and that was a child of our own.

'I remember that spring – one of my mares was pregnant and she just could not settle, always stamping and snorting in her stall and so I stayed with her as much as I could, trying to calm her down. And so it was, that I was with her on the night she gave birth to a glistening foal. But even after the birth, she wouldn't settle, steaming and stamping in the stables, and so I stayed with her through the night. It must have been well past midnight when the top half of the stable door swung open, I felt a cold blast of air against my cheek and when I swung round to look, there to my horror, a great arm was reaching in, a giant arm with a giant hand reaching out to take the foal!

'I wasn't going to let my newborn foal be snatched away like that and so I reached down an axe from the stable wall and I hacked at the arm. The great hand let go the foal, I swung the axe again and the whole arm fell down, gave a quiver and then lay there, bloody in the straw. Outside, I heard a great roar and a little cry. I ran outside, but the monster, the beast, whatever it was, had vanished, just leaving a trail of blood. But in the dewy grass, there was a little baby, wrapped in a silken cloth.

'I took him in to my wife and she fed him a bit of milk and cuddled him. By the time morning came, it was hard to remember that he was not really ours. It just seemed meant to be – as if he had fallen from the sky for us. We took him in – we didn't know what else to do – and we brought him up as our own child. But he was a strange one, that's for sure – six months passed and he was already the size of a one year old, a year went by and he was the size of a three year old. His golden hair was a constant reminder to me that he was not really ours and, you know, he and that colt that had been born the night he came, they became the closest of companions, always together. And so I could not help but remember that terrible, wonderful night when he came to us.

'Then we began to hear stories of the king and the queen who had lost their child. And I began to wonder, began to doubt, until I had to come and see for myself. And now I see him, sitting in his father's halls, now I see him sitting in his mother's arms, there is no longer any doubt left in my mind: our child is your child.'

When Rhiannon heard that, she felt as if a great burden was lifting from her shoulders. She stood up tall and she cried,
'All my worry, all my sorrow, all my trouble, washed away!'
A great smile spread across her face, like sunshine after the storm, happiness that comes when suffering is over.

She looked across at the woman who had come to the court, who had given up her child and she saw that there were tears in her eyes and she knew that her suffering had only just begun. Rhiannon took the boy by the hand and went across to her. She looked at her with compassion.
'Tell me,' she said, 'what did you call him?'
'Gwri,' said the woman, smiling through her tears, 'Gwri, for his golden hair.'
'He shall have a new name,' said Pwyll. 'He shall be called Pryderi – the one whose absence causes worry – because "all my worry washed away!" was the first thing his mother said when she saw him.'
'Very well,' murmured Rhiannon. 'Although I rather liked Gwri myself.'

But Pryderi was the name that stuck. The little golden-haired boy came to live with them at the castle, building a bridge between his parents, a way back across the cold chasm that had gulfed between them. They were a happy family, reunited at last.

It would be good to end here, with a happy ever after ending, but sadly it cannot be: there are blows still festering, a curse lingers on...

Pwyll and Rhiannon,
Pryderi their son,
Together now –
But not for long.

_vi_

Little, golden-haired Pryderi grew up into a golden, generous-hearted young man, happy but restless, always reaching out for something just beyond his grasp. And he was always to be seen riding on the white horse, with the white hound running behind them: the horse and the hound that had been born on the night that he had been born.

Pwyll grew older too, but still strong, game for anything. One day, he was hunting on foot with a spear in his hand and he found himself in a glade of trees that seemed familiar, although he didn't remember why. As he trod carefully between the trees, a white boar started out from the undergrowth. It was a strange creature, gleaming white, with red tips to its ears. At once, Pwyll was after it, spear in hand, running through the trees, letting the young branches snap against his face as he pursued it, on and on, until at last they broke out into a clearing and Pwyll saw the river and the deep pool where he'd caught the silver fish. The boar reached the water's edge and stopped, then suddenly, he turned and charged straight at Pwyll. Pwyll, his mind wandering momentarily along old paths, was caught off guard. The weight of the boar threw him onto his back and the tusk of the boar gored through his thigh. His blood began to gush out into the earth.

His men found him lying there, they lifted him to their shoulders and carried him back to the castle where Rhiannon bound up his wound and sat by his side. She tried to draw him back to her with her love, but the hand of Death was already upon him and the pull of Death was stronger. That night, she held only an empty body in her arms, the body of the man she had loved so much that she had stepped between the worlds to be with him.

In the days and the weeks that followed, Rhiannon learnt a new lesson: what it was to love and to lose that love, to lose life itself and yet, to go on living.

And she did go on living. She stepped back a little and became the Old Queen, with her hair more grey than gold, the story of her suffering and her happiness traced upon her skin. She watched Pryderi step into his father's place, watched him make his own mistakes, find his own way, earn the trust and the respect of his own people, and she watched him fall in love himself, with apple-cheeked Cigfa, the girl who lived in the house next door to the castle.

The time came, too, when she had to watch him leave, the child of her heart, seized from her side once more. He rode out on his white horse, the white hound running at their heels, riding to war. A great war had come to the land and the kings of the little kingdoms of Britain had been summoned to ride west, to sail across the sea to Ireland and to fight a war together for the sake of a woman most of them had never even seen. Pryderi rode out eagerly into the unknown, and as Rhiannon watched him go, some part of her thought that he would never come back.

vii

But mothers are not always right: Pryderi did come back. He strolled into the castle one day, as if he'd never been away. From one side, his sweetheart Cigfa threw her arms around his neck and from the other, Rhiannon drew him to her and wept to have him back home once more.

Pryderi disentangled himself from the women and laughed. He was glad to be home.

'And I'm not alone!' he cried, 'I've brought a visitor, my companion, a man who has been like a father to me – his name is Manawydan.'

He stepped aside and Rhiannon saw the man with the eyes as blue as the summer sky, the little creases and crinkles deeper now and spreading across his forehead. They gazed at each other across the worlds and for an endless moment, Rhiannon felt young and beautiful once more.

'Don't say I never think of you, mother!' cried Pryderi, 'Someone to keep you company!'

Rhiannon blushed more deeply than she had done in a long while. 'But enough of this standing around!' said Pryderi, smiling at Cigfa. 'I've been dreaming of the feasts we used to have here! I'm starving – let's go and eat!'

The four of them ate together and Pryderi did most of the talking, telling tales from the war, tales of heroics and misery, tales of the long journey home. Cigfa listened, drinking in the look on his face, the sound of his voice, letting his words wash over her. Rhiannon and Manawydan listened too, and every now and then they would catch each other's eye, and smile, and look away.

When the meal was over, Pryderi grew restless. He leant over to Cigfa and whispered,

'You know, food wasn't the only thing I've been dreaming of...'

It was Cigfa's turn to blush and the young couple slipped away into the evening.

Manawydan and Rhiannon stayed. They filled their cups with wine and went and sat beside the fire. They gazed into the flames and, piece by piece, they began to tell their stories: the suffering and the happiness and the long journeys that they had made. When the words finished, there was a deep silence, a silence of wonder and amazement. Only the day before, Rhiannon thought that she'd learnt that mortal women love once, once only and never again, but that night, she was beginning to think differently. As for Manawydan, he'd travelled a long road, fought a great war and all he'd looked for was food to fill his belly, a place to lay his head, but here was the possibility of so much more, opening out to him.

As the days and the weeks went by, a great love grew up between the two of them, a calm, strong love, rooted deep in the experience of this world. At last, the day came when the two of them, stumbling and blushing like teenagers, found the words to speak of that love. And from that day, there was no question of Manawydan being merely a visitor to their land: he was here to stay.

viii

The time that followed Manawydan's coming was one of the happiest those four had ever known. Strong bonds held them: the old couple and the young couple, the mother and son, the two men who'd fought a war together and the two women who'd waited for them. They did everything together, hunting and fishing, feasting and dancing and singing late into the night. All they wanted, they found in each other. They were happy and content.

All except for Pryderi. He was happy, but he was restless. There was something out there, out of sight, out of reach. He didn't know what it was, but he longed for it and one evening, he caught a glimpse of what it was he longed for. They were sitting around the fire, Rhiannon was telling the familiar story of how she had first met Pwyll and Pryderi heard nothing but the old words, ringing in his ears as if for the first time:

'If a king of Dyfed shall sit upon the hill,
Not undertaking it lightly,
If a man of noble blood shall sit upon the hill,
Putting his life into the land,
It will reward him with a blessing,
Or curse him with a great blow.'

All at once, his longing crystallised and Pryderi had to know for himself: a blessing or a curse, which would it be?

'I have to know,' he told them, 'I have to go and sit on that hill as my father did before me and his father before him. I shall go tomorrow!'

'No!' cried Cigfa. 'Why? We are happy here – we have no need of blessings – and suppose it should be a curse?'

But Pryderi had made up his mind. He would do as the kings of Dyfed had always done and he would have an answer to the question that tormented him now – which would it be?

When Cigfa saw that he could not be persuaded, she pouted her pretty lips:

'If you go, I will go with you. I'm not having some strange woman ride out of the hill and take you away with her!'

Rhiannon and Manawydan laughed.

'If you go,' they said, 'let us all go.'

The next day, the four of them set off early and rode across the land until they came to the foot of the hill. They tethered the horses and began to climb the hill, hand in hand up the rock-ridden, pony-nibbled slopes with the jagged crown of rock silhouetted above them. At last, they reached the top and sat there, wedged in amongst the bluestone rock.

As they gazed out over Dyfed, the golden haze moved and shifted across the land once more and hid it from their eyes. It pressed in around them and they peered out past the brightness. They could see the slope of the hill, but there was nothing. It shifted further, they could see the land below, but there was nothing. There was nothing left upon the land. No fields, no hedges, no farms, no workers on the land, no animals in the fields. Even the town and castle were gone, just a pile of stones where they had once been. The land had been laid to waste.

ix

The four of them staggered down the hill, hardly believing what they were seeing. No birds in the air, no fish in the river, no insects crawling in the grass, even the horses that had brought them were gone. The land, their land, was dead.

'What have we done?' whispered Pryderi.

'What are we going to do?' said Cigfa.

'As to what we have done,' said Manawydan, 'I don't know. But as to what we are going to do? Well, we still have our lives, we still have each other. I think we should go east, go to the borders of the kingdom and see how far this wasteland stretches... perhaps we shall find a way to live.'

They didn't know what else to do and so they set out into the east, walking in the heat of the sun across the wasteland that had been their home. As it grew dark, they came to the edges of the kingdom. The great forest of the east stretched before them. They only had the energy to gather together a pile of leaves and lie down on the forest floor to sleep.

They woke to the glorious sound of birds singing in the trees overhead. The forest was alive, untouched by the curse, and here they could find a way to live. So they stayed there and Rhiannon, who had learnt how to be queen of Dyfed, learnt now how to make a simple life in the forest.

She learnt how to bend the young hazels over to make a shelter for them all,
How to choose the wood that is best for burning,
And the berries that are best for eating,
How to gather water from the stream,
And honey from the old tree stump.

Manawydan showed Pryderi how to set little traps in the bushes for the animals and the birds of the forest and they carved out a life for themselves in the forest, living simply, day to day, hand to mouth, heart to heart. All they needed they found in the forest and in each other and they were happier than they had ever been. And sometimes they wondered privately whether what had happened to them on the hill had really been a blessing rather than a curse.

X

The summer passed happily, but as they saw the animals storing up for the hard times ahead and as the chill settled on them at night, they began to wonder how they could continue this life through the winter. 'What are we going to do?' they asked each other.

Manawydan sighed. 'We have been happy here,' he said, 'but I think it is time to move on. We should go east once more – beyond the edge of the forest there will be a lived-in land where we will find food and shelter through the winter.'

They didn't know what else to do and so they gathered the little they had and they set out once more, walking towards the rising sun, until they came to the edge of the forest. Blinking and dazed, they found themselves in a new land where men and animals worked on the earth and smoke curled from the chimneys. They walked on, until they came to a town.

'This is a good place,' said Manawydan. 'We can find food and shelter here.'

'Yes,' said Pryderi, 'but what are we actually going to do now we are here?'

'We'll work, of course,' said Manawydan, 'just as other men do.'

'Work?' said Pryderi. 'I've never worked in my life. I don't know how.'

'I know you haven't,' said Manawydan, 'but I have, and I know how to make saddles. I'll teach you how.'

Manawydan taught them how to make saddles. He showed Pryderi how to cure the leather and cut out the pattern. He showed Rhiannon how to stitch and shape the leather. He showed Cigfa how to polish the saddle until it shone and she could see her own pretty face in it. He himself took gold and made a golden pommel for the saddle. He took enamel, blue as his eyes, as the summer sky, and he decorated the pommel. It was the finest saddle that had ever been seen in that town and it fetched a high price. They bought more leather, they made more golden-pommelled saddles and Manawydan became known as the golden saddlemaker. People came from near and far to buy those saddles and, what's more, they would buy saddles from no other saddlemaker in that town.

This pleased everyone, except, naturally, the other saddlemakers in the town. There were six of them and it wasn't long before they'd got together in a huddle.

'What are we going to do?' said the first.
'It's those newcomers,' said the second.
'They're taking our trade,' said the third.
'They're stealing our business,' said the fourth.
'We're losing our livelihoods,' said the fifth.
'It's all true,' said the sixth. 'What are we going to do about it?'

'Ah,' said the first, 'let's drive them out!'

'No,' said the second, 'let's lure them in!'

'Yes,' said the third, 'then beat them down!'

'No,' said the fourth, 'let's string them up!'

'Yes,' said the fifth, 'then cut them through!'

'Yes, yes,' said the sixth, 'but however we do it, we'll be rid of them for good! That's agreed?'

So the saddlemakers began to plot. But Manawydan had made friends in the town and it wasn't long before a whisper of the plot was lifted on the air to his ears. He told the others what he had heard. Pryderi was furious.

'Let them come!' he cried. 'We'll fight them! We'll show them what we're made of!'

'No,' said Manawydan. 'This is their town and saddlemaking is their trade – we are the ones who must move on.'

They packed up their things and walked on until they came to another town.

'What are we going to do now?' asked Pryderi 'Saddlemaking wasn't the best idea you've ever had.'

'We'll make shields this time,' said Manawydan 'I know how. I'll teach you how.'

Pryderi learnt to cut the leather, Rhiannon learnt to stitch the layers and shape the shield and Cigfa learnt to polish the shield until it shone. Manawydan took gold and fashioned a boss for the shield, decorating it with blue enamel, so that it was the finest shield ever seen in that place. People came from far and near to buy shields from the golden shieldmaker and soon they would buy shields from no other shieldmaker in that town.

There were six other shieldmakers and it didn't take them long to seek each other out and soon they could be seen huddling in dark corners of the town:

'We'll drive them out!'

'We'll lure them in!'

'We'll beat them down!'

'We'll string them up!'

'We'll cut them through!'

'However you like!' said the sixth. 'But we'll put an end to their shieldmaking for ever!'

The whisper came on the air, Manawydan sighed and he told the others. Pryderi was all for fighting them.

'We'll show them what we're made of! We'll show them who makes the shields around here!'

But Manawydan calmed him down.

'This is their town and shieldmaking is their trade. We are the ones who must move on.'

They packed up their things and they moved on. They came to a third town.

'What bright idea have you got up your sleeve now?' asked Pryderi. 'I'm done with making shields!'

'We'll make shoes,' said Manawydan calmly.

'And I suppose you'll teach us how?' grumbled Pryderi.

But he got on with the task, learning how to cut the soft leather. His mother stitched the shoes and his sweetheart polished with all her might until she could see her own apple-cheeks shining back at her. Manawydan, the golden shoemaker, made golden buckles, decorated with the exquisite blue enamel. They made the finest shoes that had ever been seen in that town. From far and wide, the people came to buy them and wear them proudly in the streets. And they would not be seen in shoes made by any other shoemaker in that town.

By a curious coincidence, there were six other shoemakers in that town and human nature can be very predictable. One dark night:
    'We'll drive them out!'
    'We'll lure them in!'
    'We'll beat them down!'
    'We'll string them up!'
    'We'll cut them through!'
    'We'll do it all!' said the sixth. 'And the golden shoemaker will be gone forever!'

The golden shoemaker, however, had chosen his friends wisely and he came to hear the muttering on the wind.
    'We must move on,' he sighed.
    'No!' cried Pryderi. 'Please, this time, let me fight back!'
    'Don't you learn?' said Manawydan. 'This is their town, shoe-making is their trade. We must leave them in peace. But look – spring is in the air. We can return to the forest. We were happy there.'

They packed up what they had and they set out with rejoicing hearts, tracing their steps towards the setting sun, heading back into the west. Once more, they came to the cool forest, inviting them in to a simple life, day to day, hand to mouth, heart to heart.

xi

One day, Pryderi and Manawydan were out hunting with spears they had brought from the town. They roused a boar from the undergrowth and as it flashed out before them, they saw it was an extraordinary creature: gleaming white with bright red ears.

'After it!' cried Pryderi.

'No, wait!' cried Manawydan. 'There is something strange here.'

But the young man was already running on, in pursuit of the boar. Manawydan followed as fast as he could and he saw them crash out into a clearing. In the clearing stood a tall, round tower, that had never been there before. It had a dark doorway and the white boar was just disappearing through it.

'Come on!' cried Pryderi.

'Stop!' shouted Manawydan. 'Don't follow further!'

But Pryderi took no heed, he plunged on through the dark archway and he came out into a sunny round courtyard, inside the tower. There was no sign of the boar, but floating above his head, as if held up by invisible hands, there was a beautiful golden bowl. When Pryderi saw that, he forgot the boar, he forgot the chase, he wanted only to touch the golden bowl, to take it in his hands. He reached up for it but it was just a bit out of reach. He stood up on the tips of his toes and stretched out with his fingers. They just touched the rim of the bowl

and as soon as they did so, they stuck fast and his voice stuck in his throat. He could not move, he could not speak, trapped in the sunny space of the round tower.

Outside, Manawydan waited with sadness in his heart. Pryderi did not come back. At last, he turned and went back through the trees to where the women were waiting. 'What took you so long?' they called out when they saw him. 'Where's Pryderi?'

'We were hunting,' said Manawydan slowly. 'There was a boar, a strange creature. Pryderi insisted on chasing it. I tried to stop him, but he went on, into a dark tower, and he has not come back.'

'You let him go?' cried Rhiannon, appalled. 'You let my son go?'

'I couldn't stop him,' said Manawydan. 'There was no point me following after him.'

'Child of my heart! Torn from my side! And you, you let him go!'

'See clearly, think calmly...'

'How can I see calmly? How can I think clearly? I've lost my son!'

Rhiannon pushed past him and crashed through the trees the way he had come. She ran out into the clearing and saw the tower with the dark doorway.

'Pryderi!' she cried. 'My son!'

She dived through the darkness, into the sunlit space, infinitely quiet: there he was. As she came to him, he turned his head and opened his mouth, as though trying to speak to her, but no sound came out.

'My son!' she cried. 'What have they done to you?'

She reached up and put her arms around him. The moment her hands touched him, they stuck fast, her voice stuck in her throat. She could not speak, she could not move. Invisible hands put a golden bridle over her head, invisible hands tied a golden saddle onto her back. She felt the weight of all the suffering she had ever known descend upon her shoulders.

Manawydan and Cigfa ran through the trees after her and came out into the clearing, but it was too late: Rhiannon, Pryderi and the tower itself had vanished, leaving only dappled sunlight on the forest floor.

xíí

'What are we going to do?' said Cigfa, in a tiny voice.

'I don't know,' said Manawydan. 'I don't know.' He turned away from her and then slowly back again,

'Listen, the only hope we have is to return to Dyfed. If we can make the wasteland grow once more, then maybe, the King and the Queen will be restored to the land. It's all I can think of.'

They didn't know what else to do and so they set off, walking heavily into the west, until they came out of the forest and back to Dyfed. The dead land stretched before them. They struggled on and came at last to the heap of stones where the castle had once been. In the heat of the sun, they heaved and pushed the stones until they'd made themselves a little house to shelter in. When it was finished, they turned to the land and began to dig. They dug down into the earth, reaching deep for the goodness. Manawydan had brought a sack of corn from the town and they planted three fields of corn, laying each grain into the earth, with love and care and hope.

Every day that followed, they dragged water from the river to feed what they had planted. They fussed and worried over their fields as if they were three little children. One day, Cigfa found a tiny shoot of green in the dark earth and when she showed it to Manawydan, they smiled at each other for the first time since they had lost Rhiannon and Pryderi. Their efforts doubled – they hauled water, they tended the corn – and slowly the crop grew, strong and green and finally golden, rippling under the summer sun.

One day, Manawydan went out to inspect the first field.

'This field is nearly ready,' he said. 'Tomorrow we shall cut the corn.'

He slept peacefully that night, woke early and strode out with a tune on his lips. At last, their harvest would begin! But devastation met his eyes. Every strong, good head of grain had been snapped off and snatched away. Only the empty, useless stalks were left. Manawydan stared in disbelief.

'The grain is gone!' he cried. 'Who could have done this to us?'

He sat down on the earth and wept for the lost corn.

'But think,' said Cigfa, 'we still have two more fields.' She put a hand on his shoulder.

'You're right,' said Manawydan, 'I mustn't despair. The second field is almost ready. Tomorrow we shall cut the corn.'

He slept fitfully that night, struggling against dreams of foreboding. He woke tired and went outside. The same sight as the day before: the second field was devastated, stripped of the good grain with only the empty stalks still standing.

'The thief will pay!' said Manawydan. 'Tonight I will not rest. I will guard our last field and catch whoever is doing this to us!'

That night, he hid in the shadow of their house and kept watch over the third field. It grew dark and Manawydan struggled to keep awake. It was well past midnight, when he heard a rustling and a scrabbling and when he looked up, all around him the earth was moving, swarming with the bodies of mice, shining white mice with red ears, pouring over the land towards his field. They covered the corn, each mouse climbing a stalk, biting off the head of grain and stealing it away. With a cry of fury, Manawydan rushed in among them. He grabbed this way and that, but the movement of the mice baffled him and he could not catch a single one. As the last mice rustled away, he noticed one moving more slowly than the others and he sprang on it and snatched it up. He saw then that the mouse was pregnant, heavy with a child, but he was past caring – he had the thief at last!

He pushed the mouse inside his glove and hurried back to the house. 'Cigfa!' he cried. 'I've caught the thief!'

Cigfa, startled awake, stared at him brandishing the glove in his hand. 'What? Where?' she asked. 'Where is he, the thief?'

'In this glove,' said Manawydan triumphantly.

'But what kind of thief do you keep in a glove?'

'A mouse. I caught her and her people, stealing our corn! She's a thief and she shall pay – I shall hang her for her crime tomorrow morning.'

'But Manawydan,' said Cigfa, 'you are a man and that is a mouse. It is beneath the dignity of a man to hang a mouse. Let her go. Come and sleep.'

'No,' said Manawydan, 'I will not. I want revenge and the thief must hang.'

He reached up and hung the glove from a peg on the wall. Cigfa saw that she could not persuade him so she shook her head and settled herself. Manawydan lay down and slept patchily for a few hours, but as soon as it was light he got up and gathered together everything he needed. He took sticks and string and then he reached up and took the mouse in the glove down from its peg on the wall.

'I'm off to hang a thief!' he announced and he set out on his journey. He walked past his devastated fields, over the lifeless kingdom of Dyfed, until he came to the hill. He paused to remember the time he'd been there last, when they'd set off up in high spirits, Rhiannon at his side, Pryderi and Cigfa racing ahead. This time, he climbed the hill with grim determination and when he reached the top, he lashed together a tiny gallows tree from the sticks and the string and wedged it in among the rocks. Then he carefully opened the mouth of the glove and began to tie a tiny noose around the mouse's neck.

'What are you doing?' came a voice from above.
Manawydan looked up in amazement. There was a man with a hooded cloak, sitting on a horse and looking down at him. Behind the horse were three ponies, laden with gold and treasures.
'What are you doing?' asked the stranger.
'I'm hanging a thief,' said Manawydan shortly and he went back to his work.
'But that's not a thief, that's a mouse,' said the stranger.
'The mouse is the thief,' said Manawydan, not looking up.
'Come!' said the stranger. 'Whatever that mouse has done to you, she is a mouse and you are a man. It is beneath the dignity of a man to hang a mouse. Listen, I'll give you a gold coin, if you set the mouse free.' He reached into a bag hanging at his belt and tossed down a gold coin.

'I don't want your money,' said Manawydan, 'I want vengeance. The mouse will hang.' He began to tighten the noose around the mouse's neck.

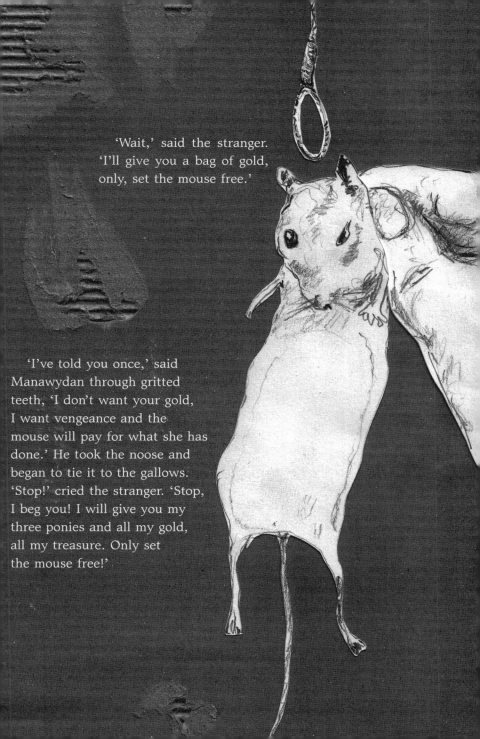

'Wait,' said the stranger.
'I'll give you a bag of gold,
only, set the mouse free.'

'I've told you once,' said
Manawydan through gritted
teeth, 'I don't want your gold,
I want vengeance and the
mouse will pay for what she has
done.' He took the noose and
began to tie it to the gallows.
'Stop!' cried the stranger. 'Stop,
I beg you! I will give you my
three ponies and all my gold,
all my treasure. Only set
the mouse free!'

Manawydan stopped. He looked hard at the stranger.

'All the treasure in the world would not stop me from hanging this mouse. But tell me this, why is it you would give me everything you have, for the sake of a mouse?'

The stranger looked at him for a long time. Then he reached up and pulled back the hood of his cloak. Manawydan saw the cold, hard face and the black hair striped with silver of the Grey Lord, and he began to understand.

'Listen,' said the Grey Lord at last. 'You know and I know that once I was pledged to marry the most beautiful woman in our world. She was tricked from me at my wedding feast and I swore I would not forget what she had chosen to do. I cursed her going and when she stepped through to this world, some part of me followed her. I was there among the people as they muttered that she could not have a child. I was there in the bedroom when the great hand reached through for the baby. I was there among the midwives when they made their oath and I made sure she suffered for her choice.

'But what I hadn't counted on was the courage and the honour and the honesty of that stupid farmer by the sea. What a fool! He could have kept the child, but no, he brought him back and the family was reunited and happy once more. I could not bear it. So, I watched for my chances and I took them. I was there when the boar brought the man down, I was there when the land was laid to waste and I was there with her wherever she went – there among the saddlemakers, there among the shieldmakers, there among the shoemakers – but I couldn't touch her any more. You were always at her side, always keeping them safe with your clever ideas and your sensible plans, and so I sent my boar once again. It was easy to lure away the boy and once I had him, I knew she would follow.

And so I caught her prisoner at last and, believe me, she has suffered, caught between two worlds.

'But you – you never give up do you? I looked through and I saw you bring the girl back to Dyfed and struggle away to make the land grow again. I felt my power slipping away and I was angry. I summoned all my people and I transformed them into mice, sent them to destroy what you had made. But last night you caught the only one that mattered to me – the woman who carries my child. I had thought my heart was dead, thought I did not care, but when I saw her hanging on your wall, when I saw your noose around her neck, love blossomed on barren ground and nothing else mattered to me, except to have her in my arms once again.

'So, I have come to you here and I beg you – I will give you whatever you want, only set the mouse free.'

'You know what I want,' said Manawydan, his eyes sparkling blue as the summer sky above them. 'I want Rhiannon. I want Pryderi. I want the land restored to us. And I want this curse to be at an end forever.'

'It shall be done,' said the Grey Lord. 'Just give me back my woman and my child.'

Manawydan shook the mouse out of his glove, into his hand. He lifted her up and she ran up the arm of the Grey Lord and nestled on his chest. There, she transformed herself into a lovely young woman, heavy with her child, sitting in his arms. And an extraordinary thing happened then: the pale stone cracked, and a smile shivered across the face of the Grey Lord.

Manawydan turned away and round the side of the hill he saw Rhiannon and Pryderi walking towards him. Above Rhiannon's head, the three birds were singing once more. They came to him on top of the hill and the three of them stood there and looked out over the land.

As they stood there, the birds of Rhiannon flew out over Dyfed. They sang the wasteland back to life. They sang the corn into the earth, the men and the animals back onto the fields. They sang the fish into the rivers, the birds into the air, the insects into the grass. They sang the town and the castle back into being. And as the three of them looked out, they saw Cigfa come running across the land towards them. Pryderi gave a cry of joy and he ran down the hill to take her in his arms.

Rhiannon and Manawydan stayed on the hilltop, side by side, looking out at the world they had made their own. Then they turned to each other, their eyes met and they smiled, a long, lasting smile.

For a while, we have been standing with them, gazing out over the kingdom of Dyfed. But all that while, you have been sitting reading, the book in your hands. Two worlds or one? It all depends on how you look at it.

With thanks to

Hugh Lupton and Eric Maddern who led the storytelling retreats at Tŷ Newydd where I first began to explore this material; Festival at the Edge for commissioning a performance of *Rhiannon* in 2003 and Ben Haggarty, June Peters and Fiona Collins who helped me work towards that first telling; Daniel Morden without whose encouragement, advice and introductions, this book would not have happened; everyone at Parthian for their help with the preparation of the text and illustrations; my parents Maggie and Tim Cawkwell for insight, inspiration and constant support.

parthianbooks.co.uk

diverse   probing

profound   **urban**

epic   **comic**

rural   savage

new   writing

library of wales.org

LIBRARY OF WALES

Independent
Presses
Management

INPRESS

inpressbooks.co.uk

gwales.com
Llyfrau ar-lein
Books on-line

The Attraction of Onlookers

Aberfan: An Anatomy of a Welsh Village

Shimon Attie

A B E R F A N

THE DAYS AFTER | Y DYDDIAU DU
TAITH TRWY LUNIAU | A JOURNEY IN PICTURES

I C RAPOPORT

howe · lls · orden · ham · oyd

SIDEWAYS GLANCES

EDITED BY JENI WILLIAMS

howe · m · boden · ladd

neale · daniel · pete · eddie · megan